Jason and the Golden Fleece
Miracle Whip

Jason and the Golden Fleece
Miracle Whip

A Different Pond

written by Bao Phi

illustrated by Thi Bui

Capstone Young Readers
a capstone imprint

A Different Pond is published by
Capstone Young Readers, a Capstone imprint
1710 Roe Crest Drive, North Mankato, Minnesota 56003
www.mycapstone.com

Library of Congress Cataloging-in-Publication Data
Names: Phi, Bao, 1975- author. | Bui, Thi, illustrator.
Title: A different pond / by Bao Phi; illustrated by Thi Bui.
Description: North Mankato, Minnesota : Capstone Young Readers, an imprint of Capstone Press, 2017. | Summary: "As a young boy, Bao Phi awoke early, hours before his father's long workday began, to fish on the shores of a small pond in Minneapolis. Unlike many other anglers, Bao and his father fished for food, not recreation. Between hope-filled casts, Bao's father told him about a different pond in their homeland of Vietnam"—Provided by publisher.
Identifiers: LCCN 2016058060 | ISBN 9781623708030 (paper over board) | ISBN 9781479597468 (library binding) | ISBN 9781515806943 (eBook PDF)
Subjects: LCSH: Vietnamese Americans—Juvenile fiction. | CYAC: Vietnamese Americans—Fiction. | Immigrants—Fiction. | Fathers and sons—Fiction. | Fishing—Fiction.
Classification: LCC PZ7.1.P5153 Di 2017 | DDC [E]—dc23
LC record available at https://lccn.loc.gov/2016058060

Editor: Kristen Mohn
Designer: Kay Fraser

Printed and bound in the USA.
010653R

For my family, and for refugees everywhere.
—B.P.

For the working class and all the young dudes.
—T.B.

Dad wakes me quietly
so Mom can keep sleeping.
It will be hours before
the sun comes up.

In the kitchen the bare bulb
is burning. Dad has been up
for a while, making sandwiches
and packing the car.

“Can I help?”
I ask.

“Sure,” my dad whispers
and hands me the tackle box.

The streetlights look brighter
and the roads aren't so busy
before the sun comes up.
Dad turns on the heater
and tells me stories.

A kid at my school said
my dad's English sounds like
a thick, dirty river.

But to me his English
sounds like gentle rain.

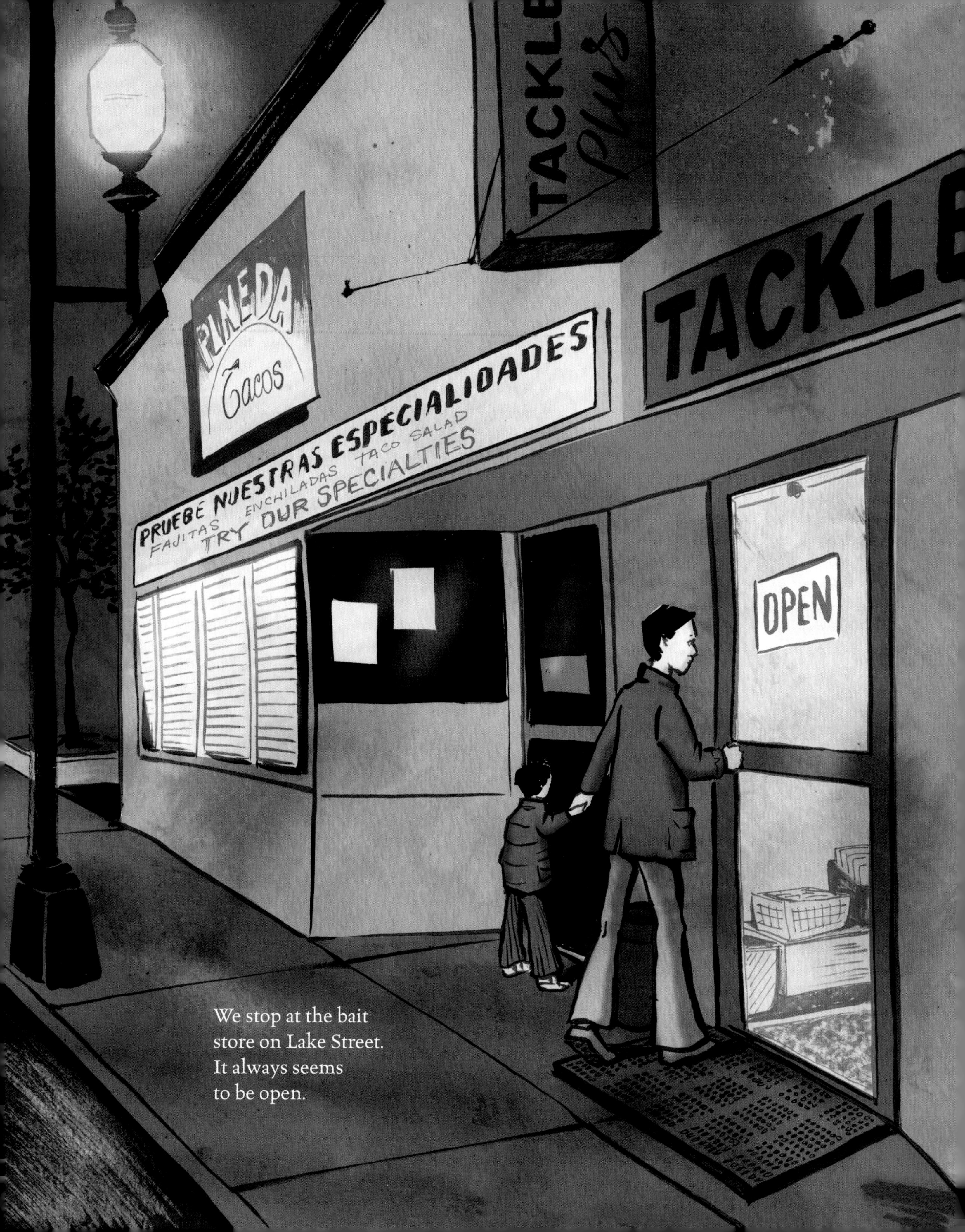

We stop at the bait
store on Lake Street.
It always seems
to be open.

"You're here early today,"
the bait man says.
"I got a second job," my dad
explains. "I have to work this
morning."
"On a Saturday?"
the bait man asks.
My dad nods.

I feel the bag of
minnows move.
They swim
like silver arrows
in my hands.

It's still dark when we get to the pond.
We park the car and climb over
the divider between
the road and the trees.

My dad holds my hand and walks ahead through the tangle and scrub. "Step where I step," he says.

I am thinking about what Dad told the bait man. "If you got another job, why do we still have to fish for food?" I ask.

"Everything in America costs a lot of money," he explains. I feel callouses on his hand when he squeezes mine.

Sometimes a Hmong man is at the pond.
He speaks English like my dad and likes
to tell funny jokes.
Sometimes there is a black man there, too.
He shows me his colorful lure collection.

This time it is just
me and my dad.
It is a little bit cold. I rub my hands together,
yawn, and look up to see faint stars like freckles.

As Dad sets up in a clearing,
I gather small, thin twigs for a fire.
They need to be dry and clean.

I count
one,
two,
three,
four,
five,
six,
seven,
eight,
nine,
ten,
and then ten more
for later.

I put some rocks in a circle
and set up the twigs.
"Like a volcano,"
Dad reminds me.

I set one end of each twig down,
the other up, leaning them in
so they rest against each other
and hold each other up.

I get it to light
with just one match.
Dad nods.

"You want to put a minnow on the hook?" Dad asks.

I want to help, but I shake my head no. I don't want to hurt that little fish, even if I know it's about to be eaten by a bigger one.

My dad smiles.
He isn't upset with me.

Dad hands me a sandwich, cold bologna
between two pieces of bread.
"Careful of the spicy stuff," he says.
There's half a peppercorn,
like a moon split in two,
studded into the meat.

"I used to fish by a pond like this one when I was a boy in Vietnam," Dad says, biting into his sandwich.

"With your brother?" I ask. He nods, then looks away.

Dad tells me about the war, but only sometimes. He and his brother fought side by side. One day, his brother didn't come home.

The bobber dips in the dark and Dad pulls.
"Got one!" he says, almost shouting.

A crappie!
And soon another.
"Can I help?" I ask.

He nods and I use two hands to help guide the fish
into the bucket. The fish feels slimy and rough
at the same time. Dad laughs at the funny face I make.

Dad smiles, his teeth broken and white in the dark, because we have a few fish and he knows we will eat tonight.
Time to go home. Dad must get ready for work. He washes his hands with a small nub of green and white soap. Then I do the same.

I look at the trees as we walk back
to the car. I wonder what the trees
look like at that other pond, in
the country my dad comes from.

By the time we get home, the sunlight
coming through the windows is just
a faint tint, blue and gray instead of gold.

At home Mom looks tired, but she smiles at the fish in the big white bucket.

My dad changes his
clothes and gets ready
to go to work.

He pats me on the back and says to Mom,
"Our boy did a good job with the fire today."
"You learn so quickly!" Mom says.
Then she asks me to help with the fish
before she has to go to work, too.

I'm sad that she and
Dad must leave, but
not too sad. I know
that later on they will
both come home.
"Look after your
baby brother," Mom
reminds my brothers and
sisters. She means me.
Then she gets on her bike
and goes to work.
I am not a baby, I think to myself.
I helped catch dinner.

Tonight, when we are all home, Dad will put rice in the cooker, and Mom will fry the fish on both sides until they are crispy. I will bring out the jar of fish sauce that has flecks of chili pepper and carrots floating on top.

At the table, my brothers and sisters will tell funny stories. Mom will ask about their homework. Dad will nod and smile and eat with his eyes half closed.

"Good fish," he will say to me.

And I will smile and nod,
and later, when we sleep,
we will dream of fish
in faraway ponds.

photo credit: Anna Min

photo courtesy of Bao Phi

Bao and his father

Bao Phi was born in Vietnam and raised in the Phillips neighborhood of South Minneapolis. He is an author, a poet, a community organizer, and a father.

Note from Bao Phi

My family came to Minnesota from Vietnam as refugees from war in 1975. I was just a baby when we fled, the youngest of six. My father was a soldier, but not a high-ranking officer, and my mom had worked at the snack shop at a school in Saigon. We lived in the Phillips neighborhood of South Minneapolis, and we didn't have much of anything. Both my parents worked multiple jobs to survive and support us in a country whose people did not understand why we were here at best, and blamed us for the aftermath of the war at worst. My father would sometimes take us fishing with him, before the sun came up — but for food, not for sport. I was much less appreciative of this experience than the little boy in this story, but now that I am a father myself, I wanted to honor the struggle of my parents. I also want to acknowledge that they sometimes told me difficult stories about the war and where we came from, including death and violence. My parents shared these stories with me, not to scare or harm me, but because these traumas were a part of our lives, and they wanted me to understand. I pass along a version of our story with those same intentions.

photo credit: Gabe Clark

photo courtesy of Thi Bui

Thi and her brother

Thi Bui was born in Vietnam and grew up in California and New York. Now all these places are a part of her. She draws and writes and teaches. Her graphic novel, *The Best We Could Do* (Abrams, 2017), is about her mother and father.

Note from Thi Bui

I must have read *In the Night Kitchen*, the picture book classic by Maurice Sendak, to my son hundreds of times. I always loved the detailed renderings of the kitchen knick-knacks, but it wasn't until illustrating this book that I REALLY saw them. I learned that Sendak collected memorabilia that reminded him of his childhood, and filled his illustrations with them. It made me feel a little sad that I don't have much memorabilia to collect from my childhood. But looking around on the internet, I've found that there ARE others who remember the same odd details that mark an Asian American, and more specifically Vietnamese American, immigrant household. The cookie tin that might contain Danish butter cookies, or Mom's sewing needles and thread. The free calendar from the Asian grocery store. The gối ôm, or hugging pillow, that my mom sewed for our beds. None of these things exactly represents my Vietnamese heritage; it's more that they add up to hold something of what it was like to be me, and alive, in a specific time and place. I would have liked to put more of these objects in my illustrations, but the irony is that not having a lot of money meant not having a lot of possessions. So the empty spaces hold meaning, too. I want to thank Bao for sharing his treasured photographs and memories of childhood, and for trusting me with them. I hope that we've managed to capture the little slice of life that we experienced, and mirror some of what our readers might have lived.

photos courtesy of Bao Phi

Acknowledgements

I would like to thank all the Loft staff past and present, especially former Executive Director Jocey Hale, who encouraged me to try my hand at writing a children's book; former Marketing Manager Lindsey Giaquinto, whose request for me to write a review of a Capstone book my daughter and I were enamored with inadvertently led to this book getting published; and Online Education Manager Kurtis Scaletta, a writer of children's and young adult books himself, who offered advice and encouragement over coffee. I would also like to thank the supportive children's lit community in the Twin Cities, especially Molly Beth Griffin, longtime friend and children's book author, who offered constant advice, edits, and support, and Shannon Gibney, for all she does for our community and for the wonderful blurb. Special thanks also to Dr. Sarah Park Dahlen for her work championing diversity in children's lit and edits to this book. And thank you to the wonderful folks at Capstone, especially my editor Krissy Mohn, who advocated for my book and worked so hard to make it better. And of course, my gratitude to phenomenal visual artist Thi Bui, whose illustrations caused seismic emotional waves to careen through me through this entire process. Last but not least, I want to thank my parents, my family, my friend and co-parent Dr. Juliana Hu Pegues, and my daughter, Sông Phi-Hu, and all of Sông's teachers, aunties, uncles, and little friends.

—Bao Phi

Jason and the Golden Fleece
Miracle Whip

Jason and the Golden Fleece
Miracle Whip